HURRY! HURRY!

Eve Bunting

Illustrated by

Jeff Mack

Harcourt, Inc.

Orlando   Austin   New York
San Diego   Toronto   London

Requests for permission to make copies of
any part of the work should be submitted online
at www.harcourt.com/contact or mailed to the
following address: Permissions Department,
Harcourt, Inc., 6277 Sea Harbor Drive,
Orlando, Florida 32887-6777.

www.HarcourtBooks.com

Library of Congress Cataloging-in-Publication Data
Bunting, Eve, 1928–
Hurry! hurry!/written by Eve Bunting;
illustrated by Jeff Mack.
p.   cm.
Summary: All the animals of the barnyard
community hurry to greet their newest member,
who is just pecking his way out of an egg.
[1. Domestic animals—Fiction.   2. Eggs—Fiction.
3. Chickens—Fiction.]   I. Mack, Jeff, ill.
II. Title.
PZ7.B91527Hur   2007
[E]—dc22   2005021120
ISBN 978-0-15-205410-6

H G F E D

Printed in Singapore

The illustrations in this book were
done in acrylic on watercolor paper.
The display type was set in Spruce.
Color separations by Bright Arts Ltd., Hong Kong
Printed and bound by Tien Wah Press, Singapore
This book was printed on totally
chlorine-free Stora Enso Matte paper.
Production supervision by Jane Van Gelder
Designed by April Ward

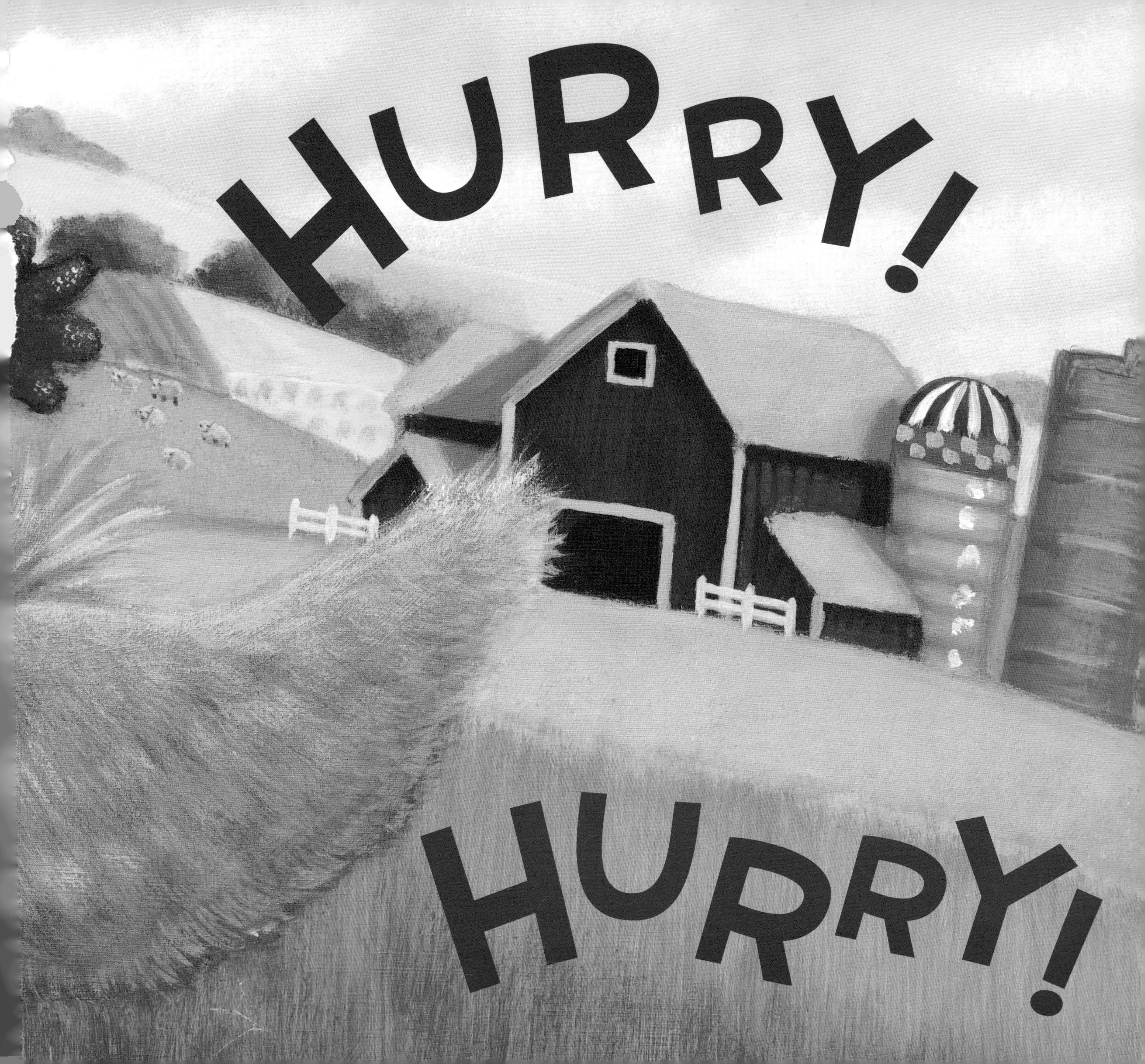

HURRY!

HURRY!

For Martha Jean, who
loves a good party
—E. B.

For my sister Katie
—J. M.

QUICK! QUICK!

Can't! Can't!

I'm here! I'm here!

Shhhhhhhhhh

Tap, tap, tappity-tap

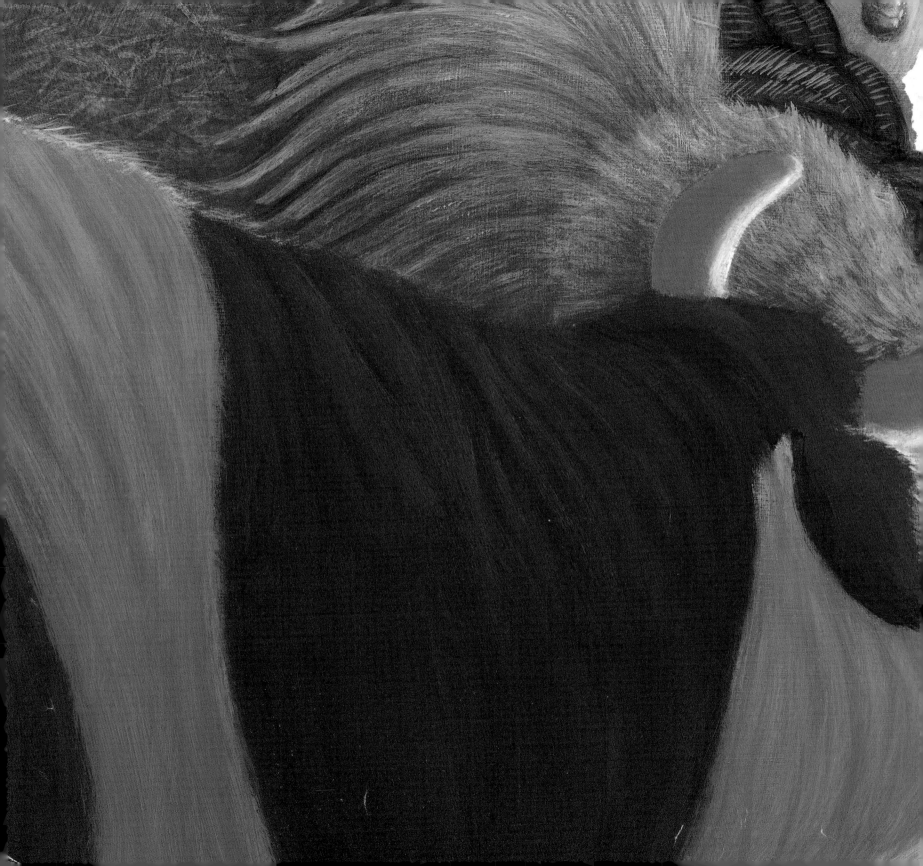

Hello, little one.